Sam the Chef

Felicity Brooks and Keith Newell

Illustrated by Jo Litchfield

Designed by Nickey Butler

It's a sunny morning and Sam the Chef is at the market. He's buying some fresh fish to make soup.

This is the Riverside Restaurant where Sam works. It only opened a few days ago. Sam's job is to plan and cook delicious meals for the people who come here to eat.

Riverside Restaurant

Sam is in charge of four other chefs. They are already all very busy in the restaurant kitchen when he arrives.

Marco is chopping vegetables.

Sita is preparing some chicken.

Lisa is starting the fish soup.

Daniel is making desserts.

There are already a few problems.

"OW!"

cries Marco.

"Where's
the fish for
my soup?"
calls Lisa.

"I need more
chicken!" yells Sita.

"I've lost
my hat,"
wails Daniel.

"You can borrow the spare hat from my office," Sam tells Daniel as he hands the fish to Lisa.

Sam goes to his office to make a phone call about the missing chicken.

Meanwhile, Marco mops up the mess on the floor.

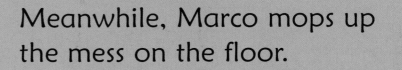

Sam puts on his apron and his tall chef's hat, then he calls the team together. "Now, don't forget it's a very special day for us today," he reminds them.

"Mary the Mayoress is bringing Pandora the Popstar and a group of important people here for lunch."

"We must try to make sure they enjoy their meal. Everything must be perfect."

Riverside Restaurant

To Start

Riverside fish soup
Chicken satay with a cashew nut dipping sauce
Caesar salad

Main Course

Wild mushroom risotto
Thai prawn curry with rice
Salmon tagliatelle
Roast breast of chicken with tarragon butter,
baby new potatoes, green beans and baby carrots

Desserts

Creme brulée
Passion fruit sorbet
Chocolate fudge cake
with chocolate sauce

Riverside Restaurant, Riverside Walk, Littletown.
Head chef: Sam Fisher

"Let's just run through the menu again," says Sam.

This is the menu that the people eating in the restaurant will see. Sam has a copy on his clipboard.

"Only two hours left," he warns.
"Do you all know what you're doing?"
"Er, yes," says Marco, "but we still
don't have the rest of the chicken."

Just at that moment
the chicken arrives.

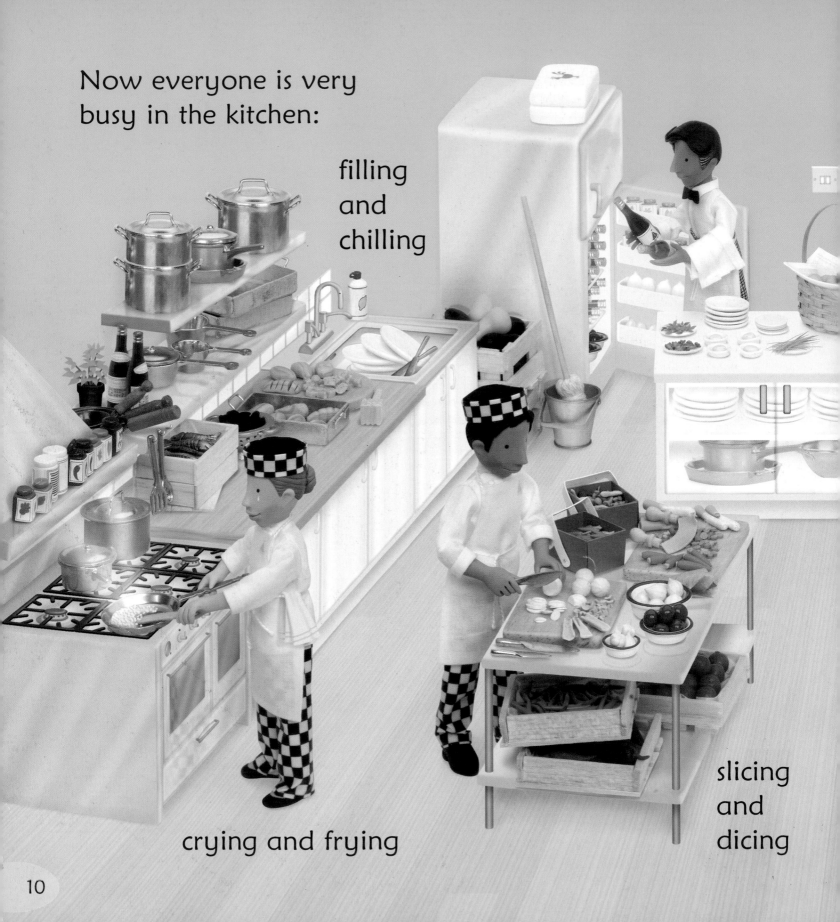

Now everyone is very busy in the kitchen:

filling and chilling

crying and frying

slicing and dicing

10

gripping, tripping

beating...

heating...

shaking
and baking

11

Out in the dining
room the waiters
and waitresses are
getting ready for
their guests.

This waiter is
polishing cutlery.

This waitress is
folding napkins.

Antoine, the head waiter, is running
through the menu with Sam.

This waiter is getting
all the drinks ready.

This waitress is
learning to balance
plates on her arms.

A little later Antoine
inspects the table.
"What is this?" he barks,
holding up a dirty glass.
"Change it immediately!"
he demands.

13

Back in the kitchen,
Sam tastes the fish soup.
"It needs just a little more salt,"
he says to Lisa.

Lisa reaches for the salt.
At the same moment, one of the waiters pokes his
head around the door. "Pandora's arriving!" he calls.

The chefs take a peek at Pandora and her boyfriend. "Looks like she needs a square meal," whispers Sita.

A few minutes later Antoine bursts through the doors.

Antoine's notepad

Fish soup x4
Caesar salad x2
Chicken satay x2

Risotto x2
Tagliatelle x2
Curry x2
Chicken x2

"They're ready to start," he announces. "The Mayoress is having the salad and Miss Pandora and her boyfriend would like the fish soup."

Lisa serves some bowls of soup and Antoine picks them up.

"Hmmm, that soup looks good," says Sita as Antoine goes into the dining room. "Can I taste it?"

"Aaaargh!"

"What's the matter?" asks Sam.
"This... ah, ah, soup is really spicy,"
Sita wails. "Oh no," says Lisa, "some hot
chilli powder must have fallen in."

"What a disaster!"
groans Sam.

Antoine serves the soup. Sam watches anxiously as Pandora takes the first sip.

"My restaurant's ruined," sighs Sam under his breath.

Suddenly Pandora is smiling. "This soup is fantastic!" she says. "The best I've ever tasted! I just adore spicy food."

The rest of the meal is a huge success.

The salad is sensational.

The satay is superb.

The tagliatelle is tasty.

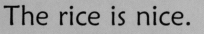

The rice is nice.

The prawns are perfect.

The meat is marvellous.

The desserts are delicious.

19

The Mayoress is so delighted, she asks to speak to Sam.

"Thank you for an excellent meal," she says. "Pandora especially liked the, er... rather unusual soup. What's your recipe?"

"Oh, it's... it's a secret," smiles Sam.

"I'm going to write about this restaurant in my newspaper," says one of the guests. "That was a great meal."

At last the chefs can have their own lunch.

"So what's on our menu?" asks Sita.
"My famous secret recipe soup,
of course!" laughs Lisa.

Chef words

Caesar salad – a kind of salad made from garlic, lettuce, olive oil, egg, lemon juice, Worcestershire sauce, croutons (fried cubes of bread) and Parmesan cheese.

Chilli powder – a hot, spicy powder made from small pods called chilli peppers that grow on plants.

Chilling – making something cool in a refrigerator.

Creme brulée – a dessert made from cream, egg yolks and sugar.

Curry – a dish made from meat, fish and/or vegetables in a sauce flavoured with spices.

Cutlery – knives, forks and spoons.

Dicing – cutting food into cubes.

Frying – cooking food in oil or butter.

Grilling – cooking food with heat very close to it, often from above.

Menu – the list of different dishes that a restaurant serves.

Passion fruit – a sweet, scented fruit.

Recipe – a list of the things you need and instructions for cooking a dish.

Restaurant – a place that prepares and serves meals for people to eat.

Risotto – a dish of rice cooked slowly with stock and other ingredients.

Satay – spiced pieces of meat cooked on thin sticks called skewers.

Slicing – cutting something into very thin pieces.

Sorbet – an icy dessert made from fruit juice, sugar and sometimes egg.

Stock – a liquid made by cooking meat or fish and vegetables in water for a long time.

Tagliatelle – pasta in thin strips.

Tarragon – a herb with a strong flavour and smell.

Waiter/Waitress – a man/woman who serves customers in a restaurant.

Photography: MMStudios

With thanks to Staedtler UK for providing the
Fimo® material for models